Sassy

Little Sister Is NOT My Name!

Sassy

Little Sister Is NOT My Name!

Sharon M. Draper

SCHOLASTIC PRESS
New York

Text copyright © 2009 by Sharon M. Draper.
Cover copyright © 2009 by Jackdaw.
All rights reserved. Published by Scholastic Inc.
Printed in the U.S.A.

ISBN-13: 978-0-545-18291-1
ISBN-10: 0-545-18291-3

2 3 4 5 6 7 8 9 10   23   18 17 16 15 14 13 12 11 10

This book is dedicated
with love
to Jasmine Draper.
To me you will always sparkle and shine
like a jewel.

CHAPTER ONE
Little Sister Is Not My Name

"Little Sister, did you touch my lipstick again? I can't find that new tube of Kissable Kiwi lip gloss I just bought. I told you to stay out of my makeup!" That's my sixteen-year-old sister, Sadora, yelling at me from her bedroom.

I didn't take her stinky old lip gloss, but I did test it out. It smelled like prunes, so I put it back.

I giggle, but I don't answer her. I'm trying something new. If my family can't call me by my real name, I'm not going to talk to them. I snuggle back under the covers for five more minutes.

"Hey, Little Sister, you got any of those chocolate bars

left over from the candy sale at school? Let me hold a few. I know you got extras."

I don't answer my brother, Sabin, either. I pull the covers over my head and screech. Why can't my family call me by my name? Is that too much to ask?

Sabin is twelve, skinny as a pencil, and I think he lives on nothing but sweets. Chocolate, peppermint, caramel. He gobbles candy all day long. Someday his face is going to be one giant zit!

Sabin barges into my room without knocking, grabs a Milky Way, then runs into the bathroom before me. I hate that!

He stays in the bathroom longer than Sadora ever does, doing what, I do not know. When he finally comes out, wrapped in one of Mom's best towels, he still manages to smell like a boy, kinda like old French fries and sweat socks.

By the time I get into the bathroom, the walls are all wet with steam.

"Sabin!" I cry. "What did you do to the soap?" It's slimy and soft and squishy in the soap dish.

"I gotta feel fresh!" he yells at me from the hallway.

I groan. The hot water is cold, the soap is untouchable, and every single towel is damp. I wash up quickly and get out of there.

"Little Sister, are you awake and getting dressed?" my mother hollers up the stairs. "It's almost time for breakfast! Hustle now, sweetie!" She's my mom — you'd think she could remember the name she gave me!

"Yes, Mom. I'm up." I roll my eyes and make a face that Mom can't see from where she's standing. She's at the bottom of the stairs. Even though I'd like to ignore her, of course I answer. I'm not crazy!

Actually, it's not like anybody is noticing I'm giving them the silent treatment. I'm pretty invisible around here. I'm nine and a half years old and in the fourth grade, the youngest of three kids. I don't weigh very much. I'm just plain teeny.

I'm the one who has to settle for the last piece of chicken on the plate, usually the wing, which I hate. I'm the one who's stuck with the last slice of bread in the loaf, the thick end piece. I'm the one who gets the last choice of jelly beans in the candy bowl. Nobody ever takes the icky licorice ones.

My name is Sassy Simone Sanford. It's not short for Sassafras or Sasquatch or something strange like that. It's just Sassy.

My mom says she gave me that name right after I was born, when she first took me in her arms, and I stuck out my tongue at her. "What a sassy little princess you are!" she said right then and there.

I'm glad I didn't spit up or something gross like that when she first saw me. No telling what she would have called me! If I had smiled, I guess she might have called me Smiley or Chuckles.

And what if I had cried? I might have been called Sniffles or Booger! So I guess Sassy isn't so bad. Actually, I really like it because it's just so me!

Anyway, I think my name is pretty cool, but nobody seems to think so but me. *Everybody* in my house calls me Little Sister. Nobody calls me Sassy, no matter what I say, and it drives me crazy!

Well, at least I'm Sassy to *me,* which is all that counts right now. I look at myself in the mirror. Daddy says I have a Krispy Kreme face, warm and sweet, but who wants to look like a doughnut?

I have nice teeth and brown eyes that blink really fast. My eyebrows are fuzzy like my hair. I have two deep dimples that might be cute, but I haven't decided yet. My nose has little spots on it. I'm not sure if they're freckles or not. I worry about those.

I think I look really ordinary on the outside. I feel the special, sparkly part of me is hiding under plain brown wrapping paper, and I'm the only one who knows it's there.

As I get dressed, I plan very carefully how to look distinctive and unique, which is really hard in a school where everybody has to wear uniforms. I've got glitter polish on my fingernails and toenails, and shimmery lip gloss that smells like bubble gum.

Plus, I wear what I call my Sassy Sack every single day — my wonderful, glorious, beautifully shiny handbag.

It's purple and silver and pink and magenta. It has a long shoulder strap, several outside compartments with buttons and zippers, and lots of little hidden pockets inside.

It has diamond-looking sparkly things all over it, and when I'm outside and the sunlight hits it just right, it really shines. When I carry it, I feel proud. I feel like a lady. I walk tall as it swings from my shoulder and softly bumps my hip.

I keep a million things in it. Maybe two million. Even I'm not sure what all's in there, but I know when I reach down into it, I always seem to find exactly what I need.

"Sassy, are you dressed?" Mom yells in that grown-up, hurry-up voice. I jump up, surprised because she called me Sassy, and amazed I'm still sitting on my bed in my underwear.

"I'll be right down, Mom. Just finishing my hair," I call back to her as I hurry to put on my uniform, and stuff my bushy curls into an elastic band.

"Her hair still looks like a tornado!" Sabin yells to Mom as he barges into my room again for more candy.

I toss my brush into my Sassy Sack, grab my homework, and head down the stairs for breakfast. Then I remember that I forgot to brush my teeth so I rush back up and grab my toothbrush. I like everything to shine, even my teeth!

CHAPTER TWO
Breakfast at Our Zoo

I gotta give her credit. Mom tries to make sure we have breakfast together every morning, but sometimes it's like feeding crazy zoo animals.

"But I *like* chocolate milk and syrup on my cereal!" Sabin says, laughing at Sadora, who is making a face. He slurps the cereal to make sure she is really disgusted with him.

"Mom, he's making chocolate bubbles with his lips," Sadora complains. "Make him stop."

"Sabin, keep your food in your mouth," Mom says without looking up from the newspaper she reads every morning. "And, Sadora, you need more than carrot sticks for breakfast. Eat a banana even if it chokes you, and drink some orange juice."

Sadora makes another ugly face, but she does what Mom says.

Daddy gets three slices of fake-looking turkey bacon from the microwave and eats them with wheat toast. How can bacon come from turkey? There's something weird about that.

"Can I have grape jelly on my toast instead of strawberry?" I ask.

Everybody at the table just slurps and gobbles and reads. Maybe I'm invisible.

I try again. "Can I have a glass of milk, please?" I feel like a tiny little bug on the floor that nobody notices. I get up from my seat and go to the refrigerator and get the milk myself.

I hate that I'm so short. When we go to the amusement park, I'm *always* one inch too small to go on the fast, cool, scary rides that Sabin and Sadora ride with no problem. I have to sit on a bench while they ride and scream and have fun.

It's the same at home. I'm too short to get my dresses from the hangers in the closet, too short to get to the ice-cream bars in the freezer, and too short to reach the milk in the fridge.

So when I go to get the milk, of course it's on the top

shelf. I stand on my tiptoes, stretch, and reach up, and, with the tips of my fingers, I grab the handle of the gallon jug, and pull the milk down. It's heavier than I expected. I wobble with it a little.

Then I realize that somebody — Sabin, I'm sure — has not put the top back on the bottle. White milk splashes all over the blue-tiled kitchen floor. Sabin hoots with laughter. Sadora giggles.

At least they notice me for once.

Mom jumps up and cries, "Sassy Simone!" in her angry voice. But she grabs a bunch of paper towels and helps me clean it up.

"It's okay, Little Sister," she says as she hugs me. I know she's not really mad. But why couldn't she have called me Sassy in her soothing voice? It would have sounded like a song.

I run upstairs to change my blue school uniform pants to another pair of blue pants just like them that are not wet with spilled milk. I guess there is some advantage to wearing a stupid uniform. At least I don't have to worry about whether the pants will match. But uniforms are *so* boring!

When I get back downstairs, my toast is cold. I never did get any milk to drink.

"Hey, Dad," Sabin says, his voice a little sneaky. "Did you notice any marks on your car yesterday?"

Sadora looks up, alarm on her face. She shakes her head, trying to tell Sabin to shut up.

"Uh, no, son. Why do you ask?" Dad is a science teacher and is scribbling notes on a paper napkin for his class. He's very forgetful and is likely to wipe the jelly from his mouth onto that same napkin before he leaves the house.

"Wasn't there a little tiny dent on the back bumper after Sadora used it yesterday?"

Sadora kicks Sabin's leg under the table. It's amazing what parents don't notice.

"I don't think so, Sabin. When you start driving, I hope you're as careful as she is. And quit kicking your brother, Sadora."

Maybe they *do* notice!

"Sam, can you pick Sadora up after school today?" my mother asks. "I've got a meeting this afternoon, and she's got play practice."

Mom manages to read the paper, jelly her bread, stir her coffee, and be aware of everybody's schedules all at the same time.

My dad's name is short for Samson — that man in the Bible who was strong and tough. The name fits him.

Daddy's got muscles better than those sweaty bodybuilders on TV. When we go to my grandmother's house at the beach in the summer, I can tell he feels proud when he struts around without a T-shirt.

"No problem," Daddy mumbles.

"Don't forget, Daddy," Sadora pleads.

"I'll be there, Sadora," he promises.

I reach back to get a hand wipe out of my bag. I use one myself, and offer another to Daddy. His mustache is covered with jelly.

He wipes, then asks me with a wink, "What else have you got in that Sassy Sack today?"

"Just my usual stuff," I tell him. "Stickers and hair stuff and jewelry and lotion and superglue and nail polish and . . ."

"Whoa!" Daddy says. "I shouldn't have asked."

"You got any candy?" Sabin asks, his mouth full of cereal and syrup.

I reach behind me to the back of my chair, reach into one of the zipper pockets of my sack, and pull out a green Jolly Rancher candy. It's been in my bag for a couple months, I'm sure. Sabin doesn't care. He tucks it into his jeans pocket. He's lucky. He doesn't have to wear a uniform to school.

"Is your hairbrush in your bag?" Mom asks.

I nod.

"Let me give that hair a boost before you get out of here."
I give her the brush and in a few strokes she's able to do
what I can never accomplish no matter how hard I try —
make my hair shine and glow and behave like it's got good
sense.

Suddenly Daddy looks at his watch, realizes what time
it is, jumps up from the table, and says, "Little Sister,
run upstairs and get my lab coat and my laptop. I'm late
again."

Of course I do it, and since he's running late, I don't have
time to explain to him how much I hate being called Little
Sister. He gives me a hug, rushes out to his car, and yells
back, "I'll see you at dinner, Little Sister! Love you!"

He wipes his mouth once more, this time with the napkin he took the notes on, and runs out the door.

Every morning, just after Daddy leaves, late, as usual,
Mom takes me and Sabin and Sadora to school.

We head for Sadora's school first. The high school scares
me because it's so huge. It takes up a whole city block. How
does she ever find her way around that place?

The only good thing about her school is nobody has to
wear a uniform. I watch the kids walking toward her building, dressed in reds and greens and oranges. So *not* boring.

She smooths her bright yellow, long-sleeved blouse, wipes a speck from her slim, faded jeans, and makes sure her daisy-flowered vest has only the bottom button fastened. I sigh with envy. She looks good enough to be on a TV show.

Sadora is really pretty. Of course I'd never tell her that. Her face is smooth and round, kinda like a golden delicious apple. Even though she's always buying makeup with her friends when they go to the mall, she really doesn't need it. She could be a model like the girls I see in teen magazines.

We stop at a red light, and Sadora glops a ton of Strawberry Delight gloss on her lips. I glance at her and smile.

"What you looking at?" she asks, smiling back. She presses her lips together. I can smell strawberries.

"If a boy tried to kiss you, his lips would slide off," I tell her with a giggle.

"Nobody's ever tried — yet!" she answers with a laugh.

She tosses me a tube of the stuff just before she gets out of the car. "Just in case!" she says.

I wave good-bye to her and tuck the lip gloss into my bag. I plan to put some on as soon as I get to the bathroom at school.

My school is next. Sabin's school is close to Mom's job, so he gets dropped off last.

Sabin just started seventh grade. He's got a face full of pimples and he doesn't know I saw him putting some of Sadora's zit cream on his bumps. He thinks he's really cute, though. I have no idea why, but even my girlfriends in the fourth grade think Sabin looks good.

As we pull up in my school driveway, my friends are sitting together, waiting. Not for me, but for a chance to talk to Sabin.

"Hi, Sabin," my best friend, Jasmine, calls out to him as they all crowd around our car.

"What's up?" he answers. He tries to make his voice sound deep.

Jasmine giggles like he just said something mysterious and important.

"I like your shirt, Sabin," my friend Carmelita says. Can she be blushing? Give me a break!

Sabin grins and flexes his arms like he's making muscles. All the girls gasp and act like he's Superman or something.

"Mom! You forgot to give me lunch money!" I tell her. She's talking to a teacher. I want to get out of there.

Mom thinks fourth-grade girls aren't interested in boys at all. As my buddy, Jasmine, says, "That's just ding-dong wrong!"

What Mom doesn't know is that fourth-grade girls are

not interested in fourth-grade boys. Fifth-grade boys, however, can make you laugh. Sixth-grade boys like to show off in the playground, so they're fun to watch. But seventh-grade boys (not counting my goofy brother) are like beings from another planet.

Mom gives me a couple of dollars, I grab my books and my Sassy Sack and hurry out of the car as fast as I can. The girls giggle and wave as Mom drives away with Sabin. He waves back. Good grief!

CHAPTER THREE

Sassy's Dream School

Once Mom drives off, my friends start acting normal again. I wait for the bell with Jasmine and Holly and Carmelita. They're dressed exactly as I am, in boring blue pants and white shirts. Jasmine has new pink tennis shoes, though. With sparkles.

Jasmine is named after a pretty flower, and it fits her. It's like she blooms when she smiles. She's never in a bad mood and she can make me laugh even on a rainy day when mud has spattered my clothes. She's short like I am, and we wear the same size shoes. I know she'll let me try on her new pink shoes later on.

Holly, who is tall and thin and has long, straight hair, does a little twirl in the school yard. She's a dancer and she never stops moving. Her shoes are soft leather with a little strap across them. She shows us her multicolored knee-socks.

"What a waste, to have to hide such cool socks under stupid blue pants," I say.

"You're right about that," Carmelita says. "At least I can show off my nails!" She's wearing bright red shimmery nail polish. "I borrowed it from my big sister," she tells us.

"Way cool!" I say with approval.

Carmelita's curly black hair bounces as she giggles. If I could trade hair with anyone, it would be Carmelita. My hair never bounces or behaves very well. It tends to be wild and fluffy, like a dandelion that gets blown in the wind.

Holly touches my Sassy Sack softly. "This is so pretty, Sassy. Where'd you get it?" she asks.

My sack always shines in the morning sun. The materials seem to catch each sparkle, every bit of shiny light from the sun's rays. Every girl in my class wishes she could have a sack just like mine, but it's one of a kind.

I smile. "My Grammy gave it to me for my seventh birthday," I tell her proudly. "She made it herself from treasures she had in her sewing kit."

"I don't think my grandma can even sew a button on a shirt," Holly admits.

I look at my sack with pride and point to sections of it. "See here." I show Holly and Carmelita. "She used pieces from a shimmery bridesmaid's dress, an old, sequined prom dress, and this piece is lace from a tablecloth that came from Spain."

"Wow."

"It's got buttons and sparkles from old shoes and hats, along with pieces of earrings and necklaces and bracelets. It's made of satin and silk and velvet, too."

"I wish I had a purse just like it," Jasmine says. She looks at her plain plastic purse.

"This sack deserves a shinier school, don't you think?" I say as I toss it over my shoulder. I look at our big, brown building.

"So do we," Carmelita adds.

"Nobody has any fashion flair in our school!" I complain. "We should be allowed to wear creative colors like fuchsia and guava and persimmon."

"I'm not even sure what those colors look like," Jasmine admits.

"They ought to let *me* design the school uniforms and be in charge of the way things are done at school! Kids would break their necks to come to *my* school," I say.

"I'd be first in line," Carmelita says with excitement.

"No blue and white?" Holly asks hopefully.

"Not a chance! Mondays would be strawberry days, where everybody — even the boys — has to wear shades of pink! And pink bubble gum would be given to everyone for the bubble-blowing contest!"

We all crack up.

"Pink lemonade and strawberry jelly doughnuts would be served for lunch!" I declare.

"What about Tuesday?" Holly asks, dancing with excitement.

I think a minute. "Tuesdays would be green days. Only green notebooks and pencils allowed. And everybody would have to wear jade-colored tennis shoes and bright emerald nail polish."

The girls giggle.

"What about lunch?" Carmelita asks.

"Pea soup," I say because that's the first thing that comes into my head. But I hate peas.

"Yuck!" Jasmine and Holly say together. They hate peas, too.

"Okay, lime Jell-O instead," I decide. "And mint ice cream. We'd work outside and sit on the soft green grass."

"And on Wednesday?" Jasmine asks. She looks excited.

"Wednesdays would be orange!" I exclaim. "A million-dollar prize would be given to the student who comes up with the word that rhymes with *orange*."

A couple of other girls gather around, listening to my imagination, so I climb up on the top step and pretend I'm giving a speech.

"On Wednesdays, orange sherbet would rule in Sassy's School. And orange juice and orange crayons and orange-flavored lip gloss."

They cheer and wait for me to continue. I love this.

"Tell us about Thursday, Sassy," Holly demands.

I scratch my head, then tell them all, "Thursday always seems like a purple day to me. Only boysenberries and grapes and other healthy purple fruit would be served at my school on Thursday. Except for the grape lollipops everyone would have to lick all day. Purple toenail polish and purple under-wear would be required."

The group surrounding me gets larger. They are listening and clapping.

"And Friday?" Carmelita asks.

I hold out both my arms like the preacher does at our church. "The sun would have to shine every Friday because that would be yellow day!"

"Yellow's my favorite color," Holly says.

"We'd have lemon meringue pie and pineapple juice for lunch. Yellow roses and tulips and marigolds would be in every classroom! And in art we'd use only yellow markers and crayons and paint!"

I can almost see this place. It's, like, real in my head.

"Tell us more, Sassy," Jasmine begs.

"In Sassy's School, all the walls would be decorated with colorful pictures, all the teachers would play really cool music in the classes, and we'd never have homework!"

The growing group of kids around me cheers, and then the bell rings. All of a sudden my sparkly bubble pops.

Dressed in matching blue-and-white uniforms, we drag ourselves into our classrooms with the cracked windows and dusty floors. I've never seen the color fuchsia anywhere in that building.

CHAPTER FOUR
Who Am I? Who Are You?

As we troop into the building, I ask Jasmine, "What color would you use to describe the walls of our school?"

She wrinkles her nose. "Tuna-fish pink!"

We crack up. "You think we'll have strawberry jelly doughnuts or lemon meringue pie for lunch?" I ask as we get to our classroom.

"Not a chance!" she replies.

Even though our school is not fancy like my dream school, I really like my classes. My English teacher's name is Miss Armstrong, and every morning she reminds us, "Fourth grade is the best!"

Of course, every teacher says that every year. I think it's something they learn in teacher school.

When Miss Armstrong reads to us, her voice reminds me of saxophone music. It's deep and rich and pretty. Her voice makes words sound like they're dancing on fluttering leaves, all magical and mysterious. I don't tell my friends stuff like that, however. I think they just hear ordinary words when Miss Armstrong speaks.

Miss Armstrong kinda looks like a saxophone, too. She's thin at the top and curved at the bottom. She smells like tangerines. I've seen the citrus lotion in her top desk drawer.

"Good morning, Sassy Simone!" she says as I walk into the room.

"Hi, Miss Armstrong," I reply. She greets every kid by name.

That's another reason I like Miss Armstrong. She always calls me by my real name. Sometimes she uses both my names.

Every day, first thing in the morning, we have language arts. I like reading stories and writing them, too. It's my favorite part of the day. But it's still fun to see how much time we can waste before the teacher gets started.

"Can I go blow my nose?" Travis asks even before the teacher has a chance to say anything. He's holding his elbow across his face. He asks this every single morning.

"No, Travis." She answers him like he's a mosquito on her neck.

"You got any tissue in that bag of yours, Sassy?" he asks me. When Miss Armstrong tells him he can't go to the bathroom, he asks me for tissue. Every single morning.

"Yep!" I pull out a pink tissue. It's clean, but it's wrinkled. I come prepared.

"I hate pink Kleenex."

"That's all I have today," I tell him. Actually, I have green and blue and yellow as well. But I give him the pink because it bothers him.

"Class," the teacher says, "let's get started."

Then Carmelita leans over and whispers, "You got any hand sanitizer in your sack, Sassy? Travis sneezed on me!"

I pull out a small bottle and she rubs the gel over her hands. I use some, too.

"Can I borrow a pencil, Sassy?" Princess asks. I wish my mom had given me an elegant name like Princess. I give her a gold pencil with a new eraser.

"You got one more in there?" asks Ricky.

"Do I look like a store?" I whisper, but I dig down and find something for him anyway. I like to be needed.

"Let's not waste any more time," Miss Armstrong reminds us.

I reach into the pencil section of my Sassy Sack once more, and pull out a purple sparkly pencil and a notepad so I can write down what Miss Armstrong says. Teachers don't want to admit it, but sometimes they forget what they tell us, so I always write it down.

Then I notice that Miss Armstrong is wearing one brown shoe and one blue shoe. They are the same style, with thick rubber soles on the bottom and a small button on the top, but they don't match.

Jasmine notices at the same time I do. She looks at me, then points at Miss Armstrong, then she breaks into giggles.

I try not to laugh, but I can't help it. Pretty soon Holly is holding her mouth, trying to hold in the laughs as well.

Travis figures out what we're laughing about and can't keep it in. "I like your shoes, Miss Armstrong," he says loudly. He cracks up.

"Thank you, Travis," she replies. Then she looks down.

"Oh, my!" she says. "It looks like I got dressed in the dark this morning! I was wondering what was so funny." Then she sits down at her desk and laughs louder than the rest of us. That's what makes her so cool.

After she wipes her eyes with a tissue, and some of her eye makeup comes off, she gets back to the lesson for the day. I knew we couldn't stall her forever.

"Today we're starting a new project. We are going to figure out who we are and write about it."

"Don't we already know that?" Travis asks. "I looked at myself in the mirror this morning, and there I was!"

Everyone laughs.

Miss Armstrong likes to answer a question with another question, especially when Travis is doing the asking. "So what did you really see?" she asks him.

"I could see I still don't need to shave," he says as he rubs his face.

She ignores the giggles from the class.

"What kind of mirror do we need to see inside ourselves?" Miss Armstrong asks the class.

"One with X-ray vision?" Jasmine suggests.

"A magic mirror?" Holly asks.

"Mirrors don't show what you think about," I say as I raise my hand.

"There you go!" Miss Armstrong says. "Good point, Sassy."

I feel proud of myself.

"You mean like stuff that makes you scared?" Carmelita asks. "Like when it thunders late at night?"

"Exactly!" Miss Armstrong looks pleased.

Travis raises his hand. "Do you mean like stuff that makes you want to barf — like when my baby brother eats the food out of the dog's bowl?"

"Uh, yes. Something like that," the teacher says. I can tell she's trying not to laugh at Travis.

"Can I write about how I miss my daddy while he's in Iraq?" Tandy asks.

"Absolutely," Miss Armstrong replies.

"How about how tough it is to be the smallest person all the time?" I ask.

Miss Armstrong smiles at me. "You'll grow, Sassy. I promise."

"When?" I ask.

"Well, not today. Be patient. Sometimes being little is a good thing," the teacher says.

I sigh. Grown-ups always say that.

"When we finish our 'Who Am I?' projects," Miss Armstrong says, "we'll have a celebration. Maybe even prizes!"

"Are you bringing food?" Travis asks.

"Maybe," Miss Armstrong says. "I promise it will be fun."

"If you say so," Travis says, shaking his head.

Miss Armstrong continues. "Let's start by talking about our middle names. Sometimes that's a good way to think about ourselves in a different way."

"My middle name is Simone," I tell the class proudly.

"Mine is Caramia. It means 'dear one,'" Carmelita says.

"Adorable," the teacher replies.

"So what's *your* middle name, Miz Armstrong?" Ricky asks.

The teacher makes a face like she just sucked a piece of raw fish. "Fair enough. I'll tell you." She takes a breath. "My full name is Queen Lackawanna Cadillac Mercedes Armstrong. My mother had high hopes and great dreams for me." She looks at the class over her glasses.

Nobody, not even Travis, makes a smart remark. I can tell he's trying not to bust out laughing, though.

Then she says, "It's okay, kids. I know it's a mouthful. When I was in kindergarten, I had a really hard time learning to write my name!"

She laughs at herself so we don't have to.

"Do you have a nickname?" Carmelita asks shyly.

Miss Armstrong grins. "My friends call me Queenie,"

she tells us, "but I better not hear one of you calling me that!"

Princess raises her hand. "My mother says I'm her little princess, so I'm sorta like you. My middle name is Butterfly." She looks proud.

"Lovely," says the teacher.

"My nickname is Caramel," Carmelita says. "It's also my favorite kind of candy."

"Yummy," the teacher replies.

"What's your middle name, Travis?" Princess asks him.

"Tree." He kinda mumbles the answer.

"For real?"

"Yep, Travis Tree Smith."

What's wrong with grown-ups?

"My middle name is Heaven," says Holly.

"That's pretty," Miss Armstrong answers with one of her cheerful teacher looks.

Holly explains, "It's a combination of my mom's name — Heather — and my dad's name — Kevin."

Now that's my kind of creativity.

"What if all of us had names made up of our parents' names?" Miss Armstrong asks the class.

Tandy raises her hand. "My mom's name is Nayla and

my dad's name is Tony. That would make me Toenail!" Everybody laughs.

"What about me? My dad is Caesar and my mom is Esther," says Carmelita. "That would make me Siesta."

"That's not so bad," Ricky says, "but what about Jack and Kelly? That's my folks' names. I'd be called Jackal!"

"And Beatrice and Stillman?" Rusty adds. "My name would be Be Still Johnson."

"Not a bad idea," Miss Armstrong says. Rusty is always out of his seat.

"I think mine is the worst possibility," says Charles Painter. He has the deepest voice of any boy in the fourth grade. He sounds like a man when he talks.

"Tell us!"

"My mom's name is Gloria and my dad is Damon. That would make me DayGlo Painter!"

Everybody, even the teacher, cracks up.

"No, I think I have the worst," Travis says. "My father's name is Mitchell."

"And?" Holly says, curiosity in her voice.

"My mother's name is Vonda."

"That's a nice name," I tell him.

"Well, if you combine the two names." He pauses. "They make . . . vomit!"

"Yeew!" we all cry out. "You win!"

"Let's try to be just as creative with your personality projects," the teacher reminds the class. Teachers always figure out how to make kids stop laughing and get back to work.

Everybody is quiet and working. Miss Armstrong grades papers at her desk while we work on our assignments.

That's when Travis gets his head stuck in a chair.

CHAPTER FIVE
Travis Wears a Chair

Travis shatters the silence.

"Help!" he cries. He sounds pretty frantic.

He sits one row away from me, so I turn to his desk. He's not there.

"Help!" he cries again.

I look behind his desk, and there, on his knees, is Travis. His head is stuck through the rungs of the chair behind him.

Miss Armstrong runs over to him. "How did you do this, Travis?" she asks.

Teachers always ask questions even though the answer is clear.

"I just wanted to see if my head could fit through that opening," he explains.

"Why?" I ask Travis.

"Just because, I guess," Travis replies. "It seemed like a good idea a few minutes ago."

The rest of the class is hovering close, not sure if we should giggle or be worried.

"Sit down, children," Miss Armstrong says quietly. "Let's give him some space."

"Get me out!" Travis calls out. He looks like a squirrel poking his head out of a hole in a tree.

"Let's try to go backward," Miss Armstrong suggests, "and reverse what you did to get stuck."

Travis tries to nod his head, but he looks scared.

"I'll hold your head and ears, and you try to pull back through the rungs of the chair. Are you ready?" she asks.

"Yeah," Travis says.

"Ready, set, squeeze!" Miss Armstrong says.

Travis grunts, but nothing happens. "Ow!" he yelps. "It hurts!"

"We're going to need help," the teacher says with authority. "I'm calling nine-one-one."

"Am I in trouble?" Travis asks. He sounds worried.

"No, dear," Miss Armstrong replies. "But I don't want you to get hurt, so I'm going to let professionals do this."

"Will I be on the news?" Travis asks hopefully.

The teacher laughs. "Probably not. Class, talk to him and keep him occupied while we wait." She hurries to the front of the room where I hear her call the principal and the emergency people and Travis's mom.

We all sit on the floor around Travis. This is better than a cartoon on TV.

"Are you okay?" Carmelita asks. She wants to be a nurse when she grows up. She covers Travis with his jacket — well, the back half of him.

He looks like a horse with a blanket on his back, ready to go to the barn.

Rusty says, "I bet this gets us out of classwork for the rest of the day! Way to go, Travis!"

I dig down into my sack and pull out a pack of tropical fruit LifeSavers. The flavors are pineapple and mango and passion fruit. I don't share those with anybody but because he seems to need it, I offer one to Travis.

"You want some?" I hold the package in my hand and offer it to Travis.

"Maybe later, Sassy," he says. He has trouble shaking his head to say no.

Then I realize that offering him candy is a pretty dumb idea. His hands are on the other side of the bars, so if he eats the candy, I will have to feed it to him.

I think about it for a minute, then I use my thumbnail to open the roll of candy and remove the first one. It's yellowish-orange, the mango-flavored one. I can't resist. I pop it into my mouth. It's delicious.

The second candy is lemon. He can have that one. I take it out of the roll, put it between my thumb and first finger, and gently place it on his bottom lip. He gobbles it quickly.

"Thanks, Sassy," Travis says with feeling. "Can I have another one?"

I eat the passion fruit and pineapple candies, and I give him the lime-green one, which comes out of the roll next.

Travis smiles. Nobody else asks for candy. I'm really glad about that.

"Travis looks sweaty, Miss Armstrong," Carmelita says.

"Help should be here in five minutes," the teacher replies.

I still want to help, so I dig down into my bag once more and this time I pull out a small handheld fan. I turn it on and it blows cool air on his face. It seems to help.

"Thanks. That feels good, Sassy. What else do you have in that bag you carry?"

I don't want the whole class to know all my secrets, so I just pull out a couple of things.

"An ink pen that writes in six different colors," I say as I place it on the floor in front of his face. "Sunglasses in case the weather is nice, and mittens in case it's not!"

"Sassy's bag is so cool," Jasmine says.

"You got any grease in there?" Tandy asks. "Maybe we can make his head slippery and slide Travis out!"

I shake my head no and put my stuff back into my bag.

"Suppose they can't get you loose?" Ricky says to Travis. "You'd have to spend the rest of your life on your knees with a chair around your head!"

"How would you go to the bathroom?" Rusty adds. "Yuck!"

Most kids laugh, but not Travis.

Two guys in cool blue uniforms, not boring like ours, rush into the room then. Their uniforms are decorated with shiny gold buttons and trim. They move me and my little fan out of the way.

The principal, Mrs. Bell, comes into the room also. She's a skinny lady with a squeaky voice. She's got a walkie-talkie in her hand and she's squeaking orders into it. She sounds worried.

"Let's see if we can get you out of there, son!" the first guy says. "My name is Leo, and you must be Travis."

"Hey, Leo," Travis says.

"And you can call me Ron," the second guy announces. "Can you breathe, Travis?"

"Yeah."

"Does anything hurt?" Leo asks.

"Just my neck a little, from where I tried to get loose."

The two guys take his temperature and his pulse, which I think is really dumb. He's not sick — he's stuck! Travis looks really funny with a thermometer in his mouth on one end and the jacket on his backside.

Then Ron tells the class, "I want all of you to stand back. We're going to get your friend out now."

Leo says to Miss Armstrong, "If you want to take a picture, go ahead and do it now. This is a good memory!"

Miss Armstrong hurries to her desk. "Oh, fiddle-dee-dee! My camera battery is dead!" she says with dismay.

Only teachers say words like "fiddle-dee-dee."

I reach down into my Sassy Sack, pull out a disposable camera, and give it to her.

"You're a lifesaver, Sassy!" she says.

Miss Armstrong snaps lots of pictures — of Travis from

the back, from the front, and with all of us around him. Travis grins and loves the attention.

Then Leo picks up a giant pair of pliers and grabs one rung of the chair. Ron does the same thing on the other side. They squeeze and pull and Travis's head plops loose.

The whole class cheers.

Miss Armstrong takes more pictures — of the paramedics, the tools they used, and Travis, grinning like he is the star of a reality TV show.

His mom shows up and runs to Travis and hugs him like he's a little kindergartner. He doesn't look embarrassed, even though Ricky and Rusty try to tease him.

His mom is so glad he's not hurt, she orders pizza for the whole class. Ricky and Rusty are quiet while we wait for the delivery.

Licking the red stuff off his third piece of pizza, Travis walks over to me. "Thanks for the LifeSavers, Sassy," Travis says. "I don't know if they saved my life, but they sure did taste good!"

That makes me smile.

The rest of the day goes real fast. We run out of time and miss math class. When the last bell rings, we all thank Travis.

CHAPTER SIX

Grammy's Here!

Mom takes me to school each morning, but I take the bus home. Since we live on a corner, the school bus drops me off right in front of my house.

"See ya tomorrow, Jasmine," I say as I get close to my stop.

"Watch out for the killer smoke," she warns.

School bus fumes really stink. Me and Jasmine cover our faces every day just in case the black-and-smoky stuff is poison.

"I'm sure the birds must hate to see our bus coming," I tell her.

"Can't you hear them coughing?" she says with a laugh.

"I think they moved their nests to the country!"

I grab my stuff, wave to Jasmine and the driver, then cover my nose as the bus takes off.

I always go into the house by the back door, but the front door is open, which is a little unusual, so I decide to see what's going on. I open the front screen, and even before I see her, I know by the smell of vanilla that Grammy is here for a visit!

I run into the house, drop my book bag on the floor, and lose myself in one of Grammy's yummy, ice cream–flavored hugs. Nothing can go wrong when Grammy hugs me. Nothing.

"Grammy!" I shout with excitement. But it sounds like mush when I say it because my mouth is deep in the hug.

"How's my saucy Sassy Simone today?" Grammy asks me when I come up for air.

"Super, now that you're here, Grammy," I tell her honestly. "How long are you staying?" I ask. I'm jumping with excitement.

"Just long enough," she says with a smile.

I know Sabin has violin lessons, and Sadora has play practice, so I snuggle on the sofa with Grammy while I have her all to myself. I can hear Mom in the kitchen fixing dinner.

Grammy is my mom's mother. That means my mom was once a little girl like me. That's hard to imagine.

My grammy is magic. Honest. When she comes to visit at Christmas, it always snows just in time for Christmas Day! Mom says when she was a little girl, Grammy was very strict and not magic at all. But I don't believe her.

I glance over at the large cloth bag that Grammy brings with her on every trip. It's a big version of my Sassy Sack, only Grammy's bag is orange and gold and black and green, and is made from cloth she got on one of her many trips to Africa. We call it her "Grammy Bag."

I think Grammy made my Sassy Sack for me because she knows how much I love to dig down into her bag for surprises when she comes to visit. In her Grammy Bag she *always* brings books and treats for me and Sabin and Sadora.

"Soooo," I ask Grammy casually, moving even closer to her. "Did you bring me anything?" I wiggle with anticipation.

"Maybe," Grammy says slowly.

"A book?" I ask hopefully. I think I have three hundred books. Grammy bought me at least half of them.

Grammy bought me my very first book when I was three months old. Mom has a picture of me holding that little cloth book with a look of real wonder on my face. I still feel like that when I read.

When other kids are bored and they pull out their video games, I pull out a book. I keep one in my Sassy Sack at all times.

"What's your favorite kind of book?" Grammy asks, even though she already knows the answer.

"Fiction!" I tell her.

"You mean books about flying rabbits and magical wizard weasels that have laser beams for eyes?"

I giggle. "No, Grammy. Not fantasy stories — I like stories about people who could be real."

"Like presidents and kings?"

"No. Like brave girls who wear long dresses and live back before toilet paper was invented!"

It's Grammy's turn to laugh. "And boys who live in the woods and survive by eating only grass and leaves?"

"Yuck! But yes!" I say. We have this conversation every time she visits. "So did you bring me a really good book this time?" I ask, snuggling closer to her.

"A really yummy one, Sassy," Grammy replies with a smile.

"Is it a mystery book?" I ask, squirming with excitement.

"It's got mystery in it, for sure!"

"What about romance?" I ask, giggling.

"Love is the most important thing in the world, so, yes, it's got a little romance," Grammy says.

Every time she brings me a book I try to guess what it's about and she takes as long as possible to give it to me. It's like smelling an apple pie baking in the oven — half the fun is sniffing the warm, sweet aromas and waiting for the pie to be ready to eat.

"Any adventure?" I continue with my questions.

"Oh, yes! A good book must have exciting activities," Grammy assures me.

I can't wait much longer. "Please, Grammy! Let me see the book!"

Grammy smiles and pulls her colorful cloth bag close to her. She reaches deep down into the bottom of it and slowly pulls out a medium-sized book. It has a bright pink cover. I'm not sure how a book can look delicious, but this one looks like it even tastes good.

Grammy places the book in my hands and says, "I brought this for my Sassy girl all the way from Florida."

I take it carefully and almost tremble with excitement. The title of the book is *The Crystal Ballerina*.

"Wow, Grammy! This is really cool," I tell her as I flip through the pages. "Look at the beautiful costumes!"

Grammy chuckles. "I knew you'd like the glitter and sparkles."

"It's just perfect!" I tell her. I give her another huge hug. "Thanks, Grammy!"

"Anything for my Sassy girl," she says, squeezing me back.

As I look through the bright illustrations on every other page, I ask her, "Do you get ideas for your presentations from books like this?"

"That's possible," Grammy admits, "but I collect stories from all over the world. I have as many stories in my head as you have bubble gum and rubber bands in your Sassy Sack," she teases.

"Well, your head must be about to explode!" I tell her with a laugh.

Grammy is a professional storyteller. She goes by the name of Sahara Senegal. I think that's such a classy name.

She travels to schools all over the country and tells dynamite stories to kids about Africa and China and cool places like that. She wears her hair in braids, makes her own African outfits, and knows a zillion folktales.

When Grammy tells stories, her voice takes me to another place and time, and I make pictures in my head about the tale she is telling. I can see tall giraffes or sneaky spiders or talking monkeys. Drumbeats make her stories sing.

The door bursts open with a *whoosh,* and Sabin and Sadora come rushing in. I guess Daddy didn't forget to pick up Sadora after all.

Sadora, the drama queen, screeches with delight when she sees Grammy on the sofa. "It's Grammy!" she cries, like she's announcing the lineup for a basketball game.

Grammy grabs her and asks, "Did you get that part in the school play?"

"I got the part! I got the part!" Sadora announces. "I might get to kiss a boy in the last act!"

"The practices ought to be fun," Grammy replies with a chuckle. Sadora blushes.

Sabin noisily clumps in with his big feet and flops down on the other side of Grammy. "Hey, Grammy!" he says loudly. "I'm going to Chicago with the school orchestra! We're gonna sleep in a hotel and I'm gonna order room service and get ten kinds of ice cream and pie!" he tells her in a rush.

"Well, that will be exciting," Grammy says.

Each one tries to outtalk the other.

I whisper "thank you" to Grammy once more, and tiptoe

up the stairs to my room so I can be alone with *The Crystal Ballerina.*

I open the book and it takes me away. I can smell the dust on the floor of the ballet practice hall, touch the delicate costume the girl gets to wear, feel her heartbeat as the curtain opens. I can hear the applause.

When Mom calls me down for dinner, I have to look around and remember that I am still at home in my room, snuggled on my favorite pink pillowcase, and not on a stage.

"Little Sister!" she calls. "Wash your hands and come and eat. We've got sweet-potato pie for dessert!" She doesn't have to ask twice. I grab my Sassy Sack and hop down the stairs two at a time.

I guess it's because Grammy is visiting, but Mom has cooked a really good dinner — roast beef with carrots and onions and green beans, mountains of fluffy mashed potatoes glistening with melted butter, and soft, hot biscuits. Yummy!

We each have tall glasses of lemonade made from Mom's freshly squeezed lemons.

Sadora eats only the vegetables and refuses to touch the meat, but Sabin eats everything on his plate. He keeps one eye on the pie cooling in the kitchen. Daddy eats six biscuits. He pretends to ignore Mom's frowns and glances at his own waistline.

"So how long are you staying, Grammy?" Sabin asks with a mouth full of beans.

"Long enough," I answer with Grammy. I knew what she was going to say. Sabin sticks out his tongue at me, but I ignore him.

"Can you stop by my school tomorrow, Grammy?" Sadora asks. "My drama teacher would love to meet you."

"Probably not, Sadora," Grammy replies. "I'm already booked at another school and I'll be there all day."

"Little Sister, can you pass the bowl of potatoes?" Daddy asks. He's already had two huge servings. I know Mom wants to say something to him, but she just smiles and gives Daddy dirty looks when Grammy isn't looking. Me and Sadora giggle while I pass him the plate of potatoes.

"So where *are* you going to be tomorrow, Grammy?" Sabin asks as he sips his lemonade. He puts ten spoonfuls of sugar in it when Mom isn't looking.

"I'm going to visit Vista Valley Elementary School," Grammy replies quietly.

I jerk my head up, almost choking on my carrots. "But that's MY school!" I say, disbelief in my voice.

"Yes, Sassy, dear. Tomorrow I will be the visiting story-teller at your school. I wanted it to be a surprise."

"You're going to Little Sister's school?" Sabin asks. "No fair."

"Nobody asked me to come while you were a student at that school, Sabin," Grammy replies. "I guess Sassy is just lucky."

"But Little Sister's school is full of silly little kids," Sadora whines. "The kids at my high school would treat you like a queen."

"Even so, Sassy's school will be my kingdom tomorrow!" Grammy tells her.

I feel like a glowing lightbulb. My grandmother is going to be the star at my school tomorrow. Way cool!

CHAPTER SEVEN

Grammy and Sassy Onstage

I get up the next morning, still a little sleepy, and really nervous.

What will the kids say? I wonder. *What stories will Grammy tell?*

I hurry to get to the bathroom before Sabin, and I change my clothes five times before I find just the right outfit — a purple suede vest, long-sleeved pale pink blouse, and my favorite blue jeans. With my sack on my shoulder, I look almost classy.

Classy Sassy. Sounds good. I twirl. I look pretty good in the mirror.

Then I screech, "I can't wear this to school! I have to wear my stupid old uniform!"

A kid who shows up out of uniform sometimes gets sent home. So I change my clothes and stomp down the stairs. I'm really sick of wearing boring blue-and-white clothes to school!

I gobble breakfast and we hurry off to school. I'm still feeling grumpy. Grammy rides in the backseat with me and Sadora.

"You know, you can wear a designer dress every day, Sassy," she tells me. "I know wearing the uniform cramps your style."

"How can I do that?" I mumble.

"Style and flair come from within. If you feel elegant on the inside, you'll look lovely no matter what."

"I'll try." But I feel pretty ordinary right now — inside and out.

Grammy wears a long, flowing purple-and-green gown, a matching head wrap, and leather sandals with little bells on the toes and jewels on the edges.

"You look elegant on the outside," I tell her as I touch the fabric of her dress.

"On the inside I always feel special," she reminds me. "That's what counts."

"I like your shoes, too. Those look like jewels on the straps."

"I bought these in Egypt," Grammy replies with a laugh. "And the jewels are made from broken soda bottles."

We both laugh at that.

On the seat next to her sits a large African drum, her Grammy Bag, and a rain stick. I pick up the stick. It's a bamboo tube, and when I turn it upside down, the little beads inside it move very quickly, swishing to the bottom of the bamboo.

Whoosh! it says. It never ceases to amaze me how much it sounds like pouring rain.

When Mom drops us off at school, nobody even notices Sabin this time.

"This is my grandmother, Sahara Senegal," I announce proudly to Jasmine and Travis. "She is the coolest grandmother in the world."

Grammy shakes their hands and greets them as if she were a queen.

As she walks, her dress even swirls like she's royalty, and her shoes tinkle with mystery.

I'm so proud I could almost pop. And I'm starting to feel that inside glow.

Jasmine whispers to me, "She has a sack just like yours, Sassy!"

"Yep! She's way cool," I reply.

Jasmine proudly carries the rain stick into the school, while Travis takes the drum.

"Whoa! This is heavier than it looks," Travis says, trying not to lose his balance.

"In some countries of Africa a young man your age would be out searching for just the right tree for his drum," Grammy tells him as we walk down the hall of the school. "The boy cuts down his tree, prepares it, then he carves and decorates his own drum. It's part of the process of growing up."

"I don't know if I could do all that," Travis admits.

"Sure you could," Grammy assures him. "I bet your drum would be the finest in the village." Travis grins like Grammy has just pinned a medal on his chest.

Miss Armstrong waits for us in the auditorium. "Good morning!" Miss Armstrong says warmly. "We are SO pleased you've come to visit us today. It was hard to keep the secret from Sassy."

Grammy replies, "I'm delighted to finally be here." She takes the drum from Travis and places it on the stage with her bag and the rain stick.

"You *knew*?" I ask the teacher.

"And you've been keeping it a secret?" I turn to Grammy.

"Of course, Sassy," they answer almost together. Both of them chuckle.

"We've been working on this day for months," the teacher tells me.

"Are you surprised?" Grammy asks, smiling.

"For real!" I tell her. "But it's a way cool surprise!"

The students from grades three through six begin to file into the auditorium. The room is buzzing with the excitement of being out of class for something fun. Several kids from the fourth grade wave at me as they come into the room. A couple even look a little jealous that I get to be onstage.

When it's time to begin, everyone gets quiet as Grammy turns the rain stick up and down a couple of times, then pats a soft rhythm on her drum.

She nods at me, and I walk to the center of the stage. I am not afraid, even though three hundred kids are staring at me. I'm starting to feel elegant on the inside.

"Today's guest is a famous storyteller," I announce proudly. "She has told her stories at the White House and in little-bitty villages in Brazil. She's been to twenty-seven different countries, she knows a zillion stories, and she bakes the best peanut-butter cookies in the universe!" I pause while everybody laughs a little.

"I'm glad she's here because she's a REALLY good storyteller, because we're getting out of class, but most important, because she's my grandmother." Everybody claps and cheers.

Grammy stands up and bows. I go and sit down next to Jasmine.

"Good morning, children. And thank you, Sassy. I'm so proud to be able to be here. Today we're going to sing a couple of songs, tell a couple of tales, and bop out a little drum music while we do it. Is that all right?"

"Sounds good to me!" a kid calls out from the back of the room. Probably a sixth grader.

Grammy continues, ignoring him. She grabs her drum and begins to beat out a rhythm. *Tap-a-pat-tap-a. Tap-a-pat-tap-a. Tap-a-pat-tap-a.*

I breathe deeply. In my mind the school auditorium fades away as the story world comes into my head.

Grammy tells two stories to the children — one about a foolish king, and another about a beautiful Arabian princess. Both tales are full of music and surprises and mystery.

Grammy pauses to take a drink of water, then sits back down to begin another tale. But her microphone is sputtering and screeching.

"Oh, no!" I whisper to Jasmine. "This is not good."

But Grammy doesn't get upset. "I think we might need a new battery," she says to the audience.

Miss Armstrong hurries to the back of the room to see if she can find either a battery or the audiovisual guy. She comes back with neither. She is wringing her hands with concern.

Grammy waits calmly on the stage. She strokes the drum with cool bops and rhythms, but the kids in the back rows start to whisper and wiggle in their seats anyway. Sixth graders, of course.

Grammy might not be worried, but I'm getting sweaty.

Then I remember! I dig down into my Sassy Sack for a second or two until my fingers find what I'm looking for. I pull it out triumphantly. It's a brand-new nine-volt battery — the exact size needed for the microphone.

I run up the steps on the side of the stage, hurry over to Grammy, and hand her the battery. "Here, Grammy," I say with my mouth away from her mike. "I have just what you need."

Grammy grins at me, whispers her thanks, and quickly changes the battery in the mike.

Without a hitch, she continues her presentation and tells another story — this one about a Chinese dragon that breathes real fire. And then she tells another tale, and then another.

When she finishes, she gives her drum one final, powerful series of bops and taps, then she bows gracefully. The kids scream and holler and cheer like they've been to a football game.

Grammy then points to me. I bow gracefully and they clap for me, too! Way cool! Classy Sassy is in the house! I feel like a rock star!

The A-V guy shows up with the battery just as Grammy finishes her show.

I get to stay with Grammy all day long as she visits classes. I even get to eat my lunch in the teacher's lounge. It smells like coffee and ink.

At the end of the day I float home because I'm so happy.

CHAPTER EIGHT
Math Class and Mall Magic

The next day I rule my school. Everybody is buzzing about how cool my grammy is.

But Miss Armstrong is back on task after the glow of Grammy's visit, and she gives us class time to work on our "Who Am I?" language arts assignment. Grammy's stories swirl through my mind as I begin to work on my project.

I dig in my Sassy Sack, pull out a red sparkly pen and my favorite notebook, and try to think. I want to write something magical like Grammy's tales.

"Can I borrow a piece of gum, Sassy?" Travis asks in a whisper.

"You're gonna chew it and give it back?" I ask him with a

giggle as I reach down into my bag to get some banana-berry-fruit bubble gum.

He laughs as he takes the gum. "I promise to take good care of it. Let me know when you want it back!"

"Please, keep it," I tell him.

Miss Armstrong, of course, hears and sees everything, but she just gives us a look that says *Get back to work.*

I think I want to write a poem to tell about myself, but it's like my ideas are floating on an ocean, not in my head. I don't know who I am. How do I write about what I don't understand?

Jasmine passes me a note that says we're gonna have math for two hours today. She's actually happy about that.

That's like the plot of a horror movie, I write back.

When the bell rings and we go next door for math class, I think time stops. The clock in the classroom must be broken. Only five minutes have passed? I'm getting sleepy.

Our math teacher, Mr. Olsen, is completely bald on top. His head shines under the classroom lights. He looks like a lightbulb.

Even though he has no hair on his head, he has fuzzy brown hair growing out of his nose and ears. I try to concentrate on numbers, but I keep watching his nose hair wiggle as he talks.

"Should you use addition or subtraction to solve this problem, Sassy?" I hear him say.

I look down at my book. The numbers are doing the hokeypokey dance on the page. "Uh, subtraction!" I answer. It's a guess.

"Good job, Sassy!" Mr. Olsen sounds pleased. I'm glad I'm a good guesser.

He goes to Jasmine for the answer. She gobbles numbers like slippery noodles.

"One thousand two hundred and twenty-five," she announces. Her voice is clear and sure. I don't think she ever feels sweaty and nervous in math like I do.

"You ready for the mall?" she whispers after Mr. Olsen calls on someone else.

"Really ready!" I whisper back. I check the clock once more.

After school Jasmine's mom is taking us to the mall. Jasmine has to get a black skirt and a white blouse because she's in the school choir and that's what they wear. Pretty boring outfit, if you ask me, but I guess it's easy to find at the store.

When the bell finally rings, I want to kiss the clock. I think it took fifty hours to get to three o'clock.

Instead of getting on the school bus, Jasmine's mother

picks us up and we head for the mall. We scramble into the backseat with book bags and purses. Jasmine has an ordinary pink plastic purse, which is cute, but nothing to call the newspaper about. I've got my Sassy Sack.

"How was school, girls?" Jasmine's mother asks. Mothers always ask that question. Every single day.

"Great!" Jasmine says. "We had math for almost two hours — really awesome!"

I roll my eyes.

"Jasmine told me the assembly with your grandmother went really well, Sassy," her mother says.

"It was great, Mrs. Cooper," I tell her proudly.

"It must be fun to have her around," Jasmine says.

"Yeah. She's leaving tomorrow," I say a little sadly. "We're going out to dinner tonight to celebrate her visit."

"That will be fun," Jasmine's mom says.

"Yes, but I probably won't get to see her again until summer when we go to Florida to visit her at the beach."

"Sassy's grandmother has a beach house, Mom," Jasmine explains. "Every morning she can get up and look out at the water."

"Maybe you can come with me next summer, Jasmine," I offer. "That way I'd have someone to talk to instead of just fancy Miss Sadora and clunky old Sabin."

"Ooh! Can I, Mom?" Jasmine asks with excitement.

"We've got several months to talk about that, Jasmine. If Sassy's mom asks you to come, then we can decide. But for now, let's pop into the mall and find that choir outfit."

Mothers are so good at changing the subject. But me and Jasmine hook pinkies and wink.

I love the mall. If I had lots of money, I'd go every day. I'd buy shoes in all the colors of the rainbow. And hats with buttons and beads and sparkles. Always sparkles. I love to dream.

As soon as we get inside, I pull out two tubes of lemon-spice lip gloss from my bag.

"What's that for?" Jasmine asks.

"In case a cute boy shows up!" I tell her, thinking about Sadora. We crack up.

We don't run into any boys at all, but it's always good to be prepared.

Jasmine is a little taller than I am. We used to be the same size, but she grew and I didn't. So I'm left as the smallest in the class.

"Here's the perfect black skirt," Jasmine's mother says in the very first store.

"But look at what's next to it," I tell them. A pretty pink skirt with gold and silver swirls sits there looking lonely. I touch it gently. "I wish I could wear something like this to school. What a waste of beautiful colors!"

After her mom buys the skirt and the blouse, Jasmine asks, "Can we go to some other stores, Mom? Please?"

Her mother gives that mom sigh that I think they learn in mommy school or something, but she lets us take a few minutes to run around.

"I need a new bangle bracelet!" I announce.

"And nail polish!" Jasmine cries cheerfully.

Just as we're heading to the store that sells those cute cheap plastic bracelets, Jasmine looks down and notices her shoelace is broken.

"Mom!" she wails. "I gotta get new tennis shoes. My shoelace is broken."

"Be for real, Jasmine," her mom says in that practical voice that mothers use. I think that's another thing they learn in mommy school. "I'm not buying you new shoes because you need a shoelace."

"You know you won't win this one," I whisper to Jasmine.

I reach down into my Sassy Sack, and pull out one pink shoestring. I have shoestrings in every color, and Velcro, too, just in case.

She thanks me, fixes her shoe, and we head down the smooth, polished mall floor toward our favorite store. Before we get there I pull Jasmine's arm. "Look at that!" I say excitedly. "A new store!"

"The Name Store," Jasmine says right with me. "What a great idea!"

I read the sign underneath.

GET YOUR NAME

DECORATED, FANCIFIED, AND BEAUTIFIED!

WE WILL TAKE YOUR NAME AND SHINE IT AND

PUT IT IN A FRAME!

ALL FOR ONE LOW PRICE!

"Wow!" I say. "What a cool idea!"

"Seems way too much, if you ask me," Jasmine says.

"I think it's just perfect," I whisper.

We stop in several stores. I buy a new pair of earrings, a plastic bracelet, and another disposable camera. All that gets tossed in my sack.

Jasmine's mom pulls out her cell phone to call my mom. "We'll be there soon," she tells my mother.

Then she notices the back of her phone is cracked. "Oh, dear," she says. "No wonder my calls have been fuzzy."

I reach down into my Sassy Sack and pull out a small tube of superglue. Jasmine's mom fixes the broken part on her cell phone and tosses the glue back to me.

"You're a lifesaver, Sassy," she says with a smile. "I'll have to take my phone in for service real soon."

We finally head back to the car with our bags of junky cool stuff.

When they drop me off at my house I say, "Thanks, Mrs. Cooper. I had a great time."

"You're welcome, Sassy," she says. "Tell your mother and grandmother I said hello."

"Okay!" I reply cheerfully.

"Have fun at the dinner with your grandmother!" Jasmine calls out as they drive away.

I wave good-bye and hurry to my house. It's almost time for dinner with Grammy.

CHAPTER NINE

Let's Go Out to Dinner

"**A**re you sure you have to leave tomorrow, Grammy?" I ask. I hate to sound like I'm whining, but I don't want her to go back to Florida.

"Yes, Sassy," she says as she tucks an outfit into her suitcase. "But we'll see each other soon."

I don't know what to do. My tummy feels like I ate a brick. Maybe if I unpack her bag tonight, she will stay longer.

"Where are we going to have dinner?" I ask. "I hope it's not one of those places where you get crayons and balloons."

"No, it's a really fancy place," Grammy tells me. "You'll like it."

"Can I get dressed up?"

"Absolutely!"

"No uniform?"

"They'd kick you out if you wore something boring like that," Grammy says with a smile.

I cheer. Finally a chance to be Classy Sassy on the outside!

"Can I wear my Sunday shoes?"

"I'm wearing mine!" she says as she shows me her fancy shoes.

"Do the bathrooms have perfumed lotion in glass bottles shaped like seashells?"

Grammy laughs. "I'm not sure, Sassy, but go get dressed in your fanciest outfit. It's a night you can be elegant."

"I like that word," I tell her. I hurry to my room to get dressed.

I choose a dress. It's all white, with shiny threads of silver in the cloth. It's got a silver belt and a full skirt. When I twirl around, the skirt almost glistens. My Sassy Sack looks great with it.

"Hey, Little Sister," Sabin says when he sees me come down the steps. "You look like a little lady tonight."

"You do, too!" I tell him. Then we both giggle. "I mean, you look nice."

I'm amazed he complimented me.

When I look at my family all dressed up in the living room, I can't help it — I burst out laughing.

"What's so funny?" Sadora asks. She's wearing gold jeans, a white silk shirt, and a gold belt.

"Us!" I try to explain. I can't stop laughing.

Sabin and Daddy, who are wearing long-sleeved shirts, red ties, and freshly ironed khakis, look at me like I'm nuts.

"We look like people on TV, not real folks," I tell them. I'm bent over with laughter.

"What do you mean?" Daddy asks, starting to laugh as well.

I wipe my eyes. "Mom's dressed like a matched set of luggage," I tell them. I laugh even harder.

Mom is wearing a pretty red dress that shows off her figure, red shoes, and a red velvet purse, but she looks like a picture in a catalog, not like Mom.

Mom and Sadora are giggling now.

"And Sabin looks like he's going to choke in that tie!"

Sabin puts his hand to his neck. "She's right!" he says. "But at least I get to wear my new boots. They feel great!"

"Nicely shined," Grammy tells Sabin as he wipes specks of dust from the glossy toes of his boots.

"It seems we need to get out more often," Daddy admits as he joins in the laughter.

Grammy, dressed in a long, flowing robe of green-and-yellow kente cloth, is the only one who looks really comfortable. Her musical-sounding laugh joins in.

"Let's get going, family," she says. "We look too good to be sitting here in the house cracking up at each other!"

"What's the name of the restaurant?" Sadora asks when we're in the car.

"The Top of the Towne," Mom replies. "It's on the top floor of my office building."

Mom's office is on floor twenty-two. The restaurant is on floor thirty-five. *That's high enough to be up in the clouds,* I think.

When we arrive, the only person in the lobby is a security guard sitting at a little desk.

"Evenin', Mrs. Sanford," he says to Mom. "Taking everybody out to dinner tonight?"

"Yes, Mr. Williams," Mom replies. "We decided to do it up fancy tonight! How's your family?"

"Doing real good," he says. "Thanks for asking. Your kids are really growing. What's up, little Sassy? How old are you now?"

"I'm fine, sir," I tell him, "and I'm nine and a half years old."

"Do say, now. I remember when you were just a baby. Do you still come visit your mom at the office when you have days off of school?"

"I sure do!" I tell him. "I sit in the corner, read a book, and pretend I'm a big-time executive!"

He laughs real loud and his voice echoes off the walls.

Sadora pushes the button for the express elevator that goes directly to the top floor. We crowd into the elevator, the doors slide shut, and I feel the *whoosh* as we go up, up, up in a hurry. My ears even pop a little.

"Wow!" I exclaim as the doors open. "It's like a different world up here."

Soft music plays in the distance. The carpet is thick and soft, and huge potted plants stand like soldiers around the edges of the waiting room.

"Are the flowers real or plastic?" I whisper to Sadora.

"Go check," she whispers back. I walk over and touch one of them.

"Real leaves. Real blooms. Real dirt," I tell her.

A lady in a slinky black silk dress comes over to us and welcomes us.

"Good evening," she says in a voice that sounds like melted chocolate. "Welcome to The Top of the Towne."

Daddy gives her our name and she checks it off on a little chart.

Then she looks right at me and says, "That's the loveliest dress I've seen in a long time."

I'm glowing.

"Thank you, ma'am," I say politely.

"Look, Little Sister," Sadora whispers as the woman escorts us to our table. "All the table napkins have been folded into the shape of a bird!"

I try not to stare. Gold-trimmed plates, pink tablecloths, and candles decorate each table.

"This is my kind of place!" I whisper to Grammy.

"Look at all the lights, Little Sister," Sabin says, pointing. I gasp.

The city is spread out beneath us. I look in awe at millions of streetlights and building lights twinkling. The headlights from cars that look like toys. I also see what might be flickers of lightning in the distance, but it's far away.

"Wow!" I say again.

"Does it make you dizzy?" Sabin asks, staring in wonder at the beautiful scene beneath us.

"No," I tell him. "It makes me feel powerful. Like this is my kingdom and I'm the queen of all that."

"I feel ya," he says.

The waiter brings us really huge menus, almost as tall as I am, with several pages describing the food and the wine.

"I feel so grown-up," I tell Mom. "We should come here every night." She and Daddy laugh.

"Hey, Little Sister, how many forks does it take to eat a hamburger?" Sabin asks me as he looks at all the silverware next to our plates.

"You can't come to a restaurant like this and order an ordinary hamburger!" I tell him. "You have to order something fancy!"

"But I *like* hamburgers!"

"You like everything, Sabin," Mom says with a laugh. "Sassy is right. Why don't you discover something new tonight?" Sabin scowls and rechecks his menu.

"May I take your orders?" the waiter asks pleasantly. He's dressed in a black tuxedo. Like I said, elegant all the way.

Sadora says, "I'll have the vegetarian plate."

Yuck.

"I guess I'll try the steak," Sabin says.

"Me, too," says Daddy.

Mom orders something with chicken. I could have predicted that. And Grammy orders grilled salmon with tomatoes. She always eats healthy stuff.

When the waiter gets to me, he says, "And what dish may I have the chef prepare for you, mademoiselle?" I'm pretty sure that means "miss" in the French language, but it sounds so sophisticated coming from a guy dressed in a tuxedo.

I sit up a little taller in my seat and tell him in my most elegant voice, "I'll have the Alfredo Deluxe, please." I think it's pasta and cheese sauce.

I try to sound very grown-up, but my voice still sounds sorta squeaky. But the waiter actually bows to me just before he walks away. Way cool!

Mom and Daddy are in a wonderful mood, laughing and making jokes as we eat. Grammy tells a couple of funny stories.

Sabin drinks two sodas, plus five glasses of lemonade, and gobbles all of his giant steak. That thing could have fed a small country for a couple of weeks.

"You're gonna pop!" Daddy warns him.

"I'm a growing boy!" Sabin answers with a grin.

I sit real close to Grammy, hating the fact that she'll be heading to the airport in the morning.

"I want this evening to last forever," I tell my family. Grammy gives me a big hug.

Sabin does his best to make my wish come true — making sure everybody orders dessert. Sadora only eats one bite of her apple pie, so Sabin finishes it for her.

He also gobbles his own chocolate cake, half of Mom's cheesecake, a piece of Daddy's key lime pie, and the rest of my ice cream.

He washes it all down with a large soda.

Finally, after the bill is paid, and there is nothing left for Sabin to eat, we head back to the elevator.

I think our whole family feels mellow — kinda like pie — soft and sweet and satisfied.

We pile into the elevator and the door swooshes closed.

I hit the button for the first floor. The elevator car starts its downward trip. Suddenly, however, it stops with a strange jerk. The lights in the elevator dim, but do not go out.

"What's up with the elevator?" Sabin asks.

"I don't know," Daddy replies. "It just stopped."

"Is it supposed to do that?" Sadora asks.

"No," Mom says, a little concern in her voice. "This is the express elevator. It's set to go from the first floor to the res-taurant without stopping."

"Well, it stopped," I say, stating what everybody already knows.

"Push the button again," Grammy suggests.

Mom pushes all the buttons. So does Daddy. Nothing happens. The lights get fainter.

"Well, family," Daddy announces with a fake cheerfulness in his voice, "it looks like we're stuck in the elevator!"

CHAPTER TEN

Stuck in the Elevator

This kind of stuff only happens in the movies. Not to real people like us. Here we are — stuck in a dingy elevator with dim lights. This can't be happening.

"I gotta go to the bathroom!" Sabin announces.

"You shouldn't have eaten like a little piggy," I tell him.

"Even piggies gotta pee!" Sabin replies. Sadora giggles.

"Is there an alarm button?" Grammy asks.

Daddy pushes the bright red button marked EMERGENCY. Nothing happens. No alarm sounds.

"What are we gonna do?" Sabin whines.

Suddenly the elevator lurches once more, then stops with a thud.

"What's going on, Daddy?" I ask. I'm starting to get a little scared.

"I don't know, Little Sister," he says. "But I'm sure that emergency button is connected to an alarm, and help will come soon."

"What if it isn't? What if nobody knows we're in here?" Sadora asks frantically.

"Well, there were still people in the restaurant, so they know the elevator isn't coming back up like it should," Grammy tells her reasonably.

"Someone up there will call for help, I'm sure," Daddy adds.

Mom looks in her purse, then shuts it with a sigh. She asks Daddy, "Where's your cell phone, Sam? I left mine in the car."

"My phone is in the car as well," Daddy says. "Do you have yours, Sadora?"

Now that's a dumb question. I think Sadora sleeps with her cell phone. She sends text messages to her friends all day long, and she never turns it off.

"How can you even *think* of not having your phone with you?" Sadora asks with amazement.

"There was a time — not too long ago — when nobody

carried phones, Sadora," Grammy tells us. "Your phone was at your house, connected to a cord." Grammy chuckles at the look on Sadora's face.

"How did you *live* back then in the olden days?" Sadora asks with a laugh. "I'd die without my phone!"

"So, do you have it, Sadora?" Sabin says, interrupting. "I really gotta go bad!"

"It *never* leaves my purse. I'll save us." Sadora speaks with confidence.

She digs down into her purse, a cute little designer thing — not a cool sack like mine — and pulls out her phone. It's pink with little pearls around the edge. I want one just like it, but Mom won't let me have one yet.

She flips it open, then frowns at it like it's some kind of alien weapon. "There's no signal," she says. "Nothing."

She looks lost and confused, as if her best friend had just moved to another country.

Grammy speaks up. "Well, if we can't get out right away, let's make the most of it. Let's sit down on the floor, make ourselves comfortable, and I'll tell stories to keep us occupied."

But surprisingly nobody seems to like Grammy's idea. Everybody wants out — right away.

"The floor is dirty," Sadora whines. "I don't want to get my new outfit messed up. Isn't there another way out of here?"

"And I *really* gotta go to the bathroom!" Sabin cries, hopping from one foot to the other.

"Did you push the DOOR OPEN button, Daddy?" I ask.

"I pushed all of them," he answers, irritation in his voice. But he presses it once again.

This time, like an animal taking a deep breath, the door slides open — just a little, and way out of whack. It shudders and stops once more, like it's done all it can do.

"Hooray!" Sabin cries out.

A small opening is gaping at us. It's really skinny, not even one foot wide. I can see the carpeted hall on the floor where the elevator has stopped.

It's not lined up evenly like elevators are supposed to do. But the hall is clearly out there, and a bathroom for Sabin is probably very close.

The hallway is not brightly lit like it usually is when I visit Mom's office. The lights are very dim.

"Can you peek through it, Sam?" Mom asks.

"I can see very little," he answers. "It looks like emergency generators are lighting the hallway."

"Is *anybody* out there?" Daddy calls loudly. No one answers.

"Hey! Help!" Sabin yells. "Where *is* everybody?"

He, too, is answered only by silence.

I reach down in my Sassy Sack and pull out a skinny little flashlight that I won at a carnival last summer. I hand it to Daddy.

"Perfect, Sassy!" Daddy says, sounding really pleased as he takes the flashlight. "You always seem to have just the right thing down in that bag of yours."

I guess the stress of the situation makes him remember my name. But I don't say anything.

Daddy clicks on the flashlight and shines it through the hole.

"I can see the number twenty-two on the side of the elevator door," Daddy reports.

"That's my floor!" Mom says excitedly. "My office is two doors down on the left, and the security stand is just beyond that. Mr. Williams makes night rounds of every floor all night long."

"Let me see if I can squeeze through," Daddy says, trying to take charge. He can only fit his arm through the opening.

"Daddy, that opening is too small and you are way too big," I tell him.

"I told you to cut back on the biscuits," Mom teases.

"It's not the biscuits, it's the huge muscles," Daddy replies with a grin, flexing his arm like those guys on bodybuilding shows. "Can *you* get through, Susan?" he asks Mom.

"You've got me there!" Mom replies. "Even if I suck in everything, there's no way I can fit."

Grammy says, "Well, it's clear that Sadora and Sabin are too large as well. Actually, none of us is small enough to fit through that hole — no one except Sassy. She's tiny like a little mouse."

"Me?" I ask. This time my voice really does come out as a squeak.

"I'm not letting my baby risk her life!" Mom says right away. "We'll just wait for help to arrive. It can't be much longer."

Mom touches my hair gently. That makes me feel good.

"Risk my life?" I whisper. I'm not so sure about this.

"She might get dirty, but she's in no danger," my father explains.

"Please let her try," Sabin pleads. "I'm gonna explode."

"Sit down, Sabin," Grammy suggests. "Think about sand, about a dusty, dry day."

Sabin sits down, but he looks real uncomfortable. His face almost begs me.

"I can do it, Mom," I tell her. I think I sound braver than I feel.

"No, sweetie. I don't want you to do this." Mom sounds a little scared. She looks at Daddy. "What do you think, Sam?"

"All she has to do is slip through the door like a little snake and run like a bunny to get help."

Why is he comparing me to forest animals?

But he doesn't sound sure. I like it when Daddy sounds like he knows what he's talking about. Fathers should not sound shaky.

"What about the door?" Mom asks. "What if it closes suddenly?"

"She'll be a pancake," Sabin says.

He can't help teasing me, even when he's in trouble.

"Give me your shoes," I tell Sabin suddenly.

"Why?" he asks.

"Do you want me to get help or not?" I tell him with my hand on my hip.

"Sure I do," he says.

"Aren't those steel-toed boots?" I ask Mom.

"Yes, they are," Mom replies. "We just bought them last week."

Sabin unties his boots, slips them off his feet, and hands them to me, frowning. I don't make a joke about his stinky feet, but I could have.

"What's your plan, Sassy?" Grammy asks.

"I'm going to use Sabin's boots to make sure the door stays open," I explain.

I take the boots and jam them into the small opening.

"You're getting them all scratched up," Sabin complains.

"Do you see a toilet in this elevator car?" I ask him.

Sabin gets quiet.

Daddy says, "There is no electricity. The doors are not going to close. But the boots are a great idea, just in case."

"You're a genius, Little Sister," Sadora says with admiration in her voice.

"I've been to Mom's office a million times," I tell them. "I'll run down there, pick up the phone, and call nine-one-one. It should take me three minutes."

"Can you do it in two?" Sabin pleads. He really looks pitiful. I feel sorry for him.

Grammy smiles at me with confidence. "You're going to be our champion, Sassy," she says with pride in her voice.

"You're pretty brave, Little Sister," Sadora admits. "Aren't you scared?"

I take a deep breath. "The door can't hurt me, and the dark can't get me. I'm cool!"

I don't tell Sadora that I'm a teeny bit scared of the dark.

I like the way she looks at me like I'm a big deal instead of a little nobody.

Daddy asks me, "Are you sure, Little Sister?"

"Sure!" I say. "Let me do this before Sabin explodes!" Everybody, except for Sabin, cracks up.

Daddy and Mom hug me tight, and Grammy kisses me on the forehead. Daddy hands me the flashlight, and Mom gives me the key to her office.

I'm ready. Then I decide I need to say something before I go.

"Wait!" I tell them all.

They all look at me in the dim light. "What's wrong?" Mom asks.

"Nothing's wrong. But can I ask you guys something?"

"What?" Sabin asks. He's wiggling again.

"It drives me crazy when you call me Little Sister all the time. When I get back, can you guys call me Sassy sometimes?" I look at them with hope.

Sadora starts to laugh. "Why didn't you say something sooner?" she asks. "I didn't know it bothered you so much."

"Really?" I'm stunned. In the dim light I give her my biggest smile.

"Is that all?" Sabin asks. "Now can we hurry this along? Thinking about sandy deserts isn't working very well."

CHAPTER ELEVEN

Can Sassy Save the Day?

Everybody laughs again, and Daddy hugs me once more. I toss my sack through the opening first, turn myself sideways, suck in my breath, then I slip through the doorway like a puff of smoke. I fit perfectly.

I wonder if my dress is getting dirty. It's so dark I can't tell.

I look around. Everything is darker than it should be. Where are the lights? Really strange.

"I'm okay," I call back to them. "I'm going to Mom's office now. Hang in there, Sabin!"

"Hurry!" I hear him call.

I switch on the flashlight and tiptoe down the hall toward Mom's office. Why are all the main lights off? Only those pale generator lights that Daddy talked about are glowing. Even at night the halls of an office building should be well lit. Right?

My heart is thudding.

I find Mom's office with no trouble, use my flashlight to see what I'm doing, put Mom's key in the lock, and open the door to her office.

I have to adjust my eyes a minute and blink. When I look out the big wide picture window, instead of seeing the lights of the city twinkling like they had been while we were in the restaurant, all I can see is darkness.

"It's like somebody has blown out all the candles!" I whisper.

I see headlights and the red taillights of cars, but mostly the city looks like it's been covered with a dark blanket. The biggest light is coming from the full moon and the twinkling stars.

"What's going on?" I wonder out loud.

I reach for the phone on Mom's desk and pick it up. But just like Sadora's cell phone, the line is silent.

"Maybe Martians have taken over the planet!" I keep talking out loud. I hope I don't sound crazy.

"No, that only happens in movies," I tell myself. "So what's causing the lights to be out?"

There is no one around to answer me.

"This is really spooky," I whisper.

I leave Mom's office, and walk toward the security-guard stand on her floor. My little carnival flashlight doesn't help much, but I can see okay.

My steps seem to echo and the flashlight is making weird shadows.

"Enough of this!" I whisper. "I want my mother."

Suddenly the light of a really powerful flashlight shines directly in my face. I almost scream.

"Who's there?" a loud voice bellows.

I recognize his voice and sigh with relief.

"It's me, Mr. Williams. Sassy Sanford," I say. "I'm Susan's daughter, remember?"

He probably thinks I'm really scared. He's right.

He takes the light out of my eyes and says gently, "Sassy? What are you doing here all alone? Where is your family?"

"They're trapped in the elevator!" I shout. I am so relieved I almost wet my pants.

"Oh, my!" he says.

"What happened to all the lights?" I demand.

"We had a major power outage a few minutes ago," he explains. "The whole city got blacked out. Pow! Lights out everywhere!"

"Why?" I ask. I'm still thinking about the possibility of space invaders.

"According to the reports I've been getting from my two-way radio," he tells me, "lightning struck a couple of the major power stations."

"Lightning? That's crazy."

"Yep. And all the rest of the power stations shut down in response. Even the cell phone towers clicked off. The system is designed to do that for safety purposes."

"Safety?" I repeat. "That's not safe, that's dumb! My family is stuck in an elevator because of that!"

"Well, let's go see if we can get them out, little lady!" Mr. Williams says. His voice is full of confidence. I relax a little.

He speaks into his walkie-talkie and alerts the police. "Family stuck in elevator on the twenty-second floor of the Tower Building," he says. "Send units to this location right away."

Then we hurry down the hall and back to the elevator. The narrow opening I had crawled through is still there. So are Sabin's boots.

"Mom! Daddy! I found Mr. Williams!" I call to them. "He says the whole city is blacked out — no power, no phones anywhere!"

"Oh, no!" I hear Sabin cry out.

"Can you get the elevator started from that end, Mr. Williams?" I hear Mom ask.

"Sorry, ma'am. Automatic shutdown. But I've called a rescue squad and they'll be here shortly. Is everyone okay in there?"

"We're fine, sir," Daddy's voice replies. "My son needs to find a bathroom pretty soon, but other than that, we're all safe."

"Your daughter here is a hero!" Mr. Williams exclaims. "If she hadn't been small enough to squeeze through that opening, you all would probably have been in there for hours!"

I can hear Sabin groan. I try not to laugh.

Considering there are probably lots of really serious emergencies tonight, the rescue team from the fire department arrives really quickly.

The firefighters wear their serious working gear — bright yellow uniforms made of some kind of stuff that I guess doesn't burn, and helmets and hatchets and ropes.

One guy carries an oxygen tank and another firefighter — a woman — carries one of those funny-looking tools that had been used to get Travis out of the chair.

"How did you get up here?" I ask the woman.

"The stairs," she answers.

"You walked up twenty-two floors?" I ask.

"Actually, when we heard a family was trapped, we *ran* up the stairs!"

"Wow," I say. "Way cool. Thanks."

"Are you okay?" she asks. "My name is Rosa, and that's Big Bob over there."

"I'm fine," I tell her. "It's my family that needs help. And my brother has to go to the bathroom."

Rosa and Big Bob hurry over to the elevator door and get to work. It's all over in a few minutes. They pry the door open with the equipment, and, like a burp, Sabin explodes out of the enlarged opening.

Even though he only has on socks, he runs so fast down the hall to the bathroom that he could make the Olympic track team. The firefighters chuckle at his run, then carefully help Grammy, Mom, Sadora, and Daddy out of the elevator.

By the time the firefighters are packing up their gear, and my family are all standing in the hall looking a little embarrassed, Sabin walks back to us — slowly this time.

"Feel better, son?" Daddy asks.

"Oh, yeah!" Sabin says, exhaling with relief. "Thanks, Little Sist — uh, I mean, Sassy," he says. "I couldn't have held out one second longer!"

We all crack up. Sadora starts the laughter, then Sabin giggles, laughing at himself. Then Mom and Daddy and Grammy join in, and we sound like the laugh track to a television comedy show.

Wiping his eyes, Daddy says to Rosa and Big Bob, "We really thank you for taking the time to rescue us. We know you have lots more calls to answer tonight."

"Your family is lucky that you had someone small enough to get out and call for help," Rosa says.

Everybody looks at me and smiles again. I feel really special.

"I *really* want to thank you," Sabin says. "Another few minutes and I would have exploded!"

Rosa laughs. "It's our pleasure, son."

"Does your family need assistance down the stairs?" Big Bob asks Daddy.

"No, thanks. We're fine," Daddy says. "Go and do what you need to do for others."

Big Bob and Rosa hurry on to their next emergency. The hall is suddenly dark and silent once more.

Our whole family, along with Mr. Williams, walks slowly back to Mom's office. The storm has passed. The city, lit only by moonlight and stars, looks quiet and sleepy.

"The cars on the road seem like they're lost," Sabin says. "As if they don't belong there or something."

No one else says much — it's a really strange sight.

Then, as suddenly as they had gone out, the lights begin to flicker back on. The computer in Mom's office buzzes and hums, and the lights sputter back to life.

The lights below in the city blink once or twice, as if they are waking up.

Then, like somebody is flicking a switch, the whole city bursts back into life. Streetlights. Red and green lights. Neon signs. Buildings and houses. Brightly shining once again.

We all cheer.

"Well, this is certainly an evening we'll always remember!" Grammy says. "This is a great story to add to my collection!"

"I'm just thankful we're all safe," Mom says.

"And that I didn't embarrass myself!" Sabin adds.

"And that my cell phone is working again!" Sadora declares cheerfully.

"My dress got all dirty!" I announce sadly.

"Remember what I told you, Sassy," Grammy reminds me. "It's what inside that counts."

"I think I get it now," I tell her.

"Well, we're all really thankful that our Sassy, our baby girl who we love so much, was little enough to save us all!" Daddy says with pride.

"You know what?" I tell everyone, admitting something I'm just figuring out. "I really don't mind being called Little Sister sometimes. It means something special now. I'm glad I was little enough to get through that door."

They all hug me then, one of those group hugs like you see on TV comedy shows, but this is very real, and way cool.

We leave Mom's office and head back down the hall. We look to our right, where the elevator is now working and waiting for us, and to the left, where the staircase is. We take the stairs!

CHAPTER TWELVE
Cameras and Questions

I'm the first to get to the bottom of the stairs. Whew! That was a *lot* of steps! I push open the doors of the building and I'm almost blinded from blinking and flashing lights in my eyes. I don't get it. Cameras?

A lady reporter hurries over to me. I have seen her on the six o'clock news. "Are you the one who saved your family?" she asks. She looks excited. I'm not sure why.

"I guess so," I tell her.

Somebody snaps my picture again. I look down and realize my pretty white dress is dirty. My hair is a mess. This is *not* a good time to have a photo taken.

I dig down into my Sassy Sack and pull out a brush and a pink hair band. I don't think either one helps very much.

By this time the rest of the family comes outside. The news crew seems to confuse them also.

"What's up?" Sadora asks me as she fixes her hair and puts on lipstick. "After all, we're just an overdressed, over-stuffed family who got stuck in an elevator with a kid who had too much to eat and drink."

I giggle. "You're right!"

Sabin has put his shoes back on. He looks a little embarrassed.

"What is your name, sir?" the reporter lady asks Daddy.

"Samson Sanford. Why are reporters gathered here? Is someone hurt?" Daddy holds my hand.

"We heard about how a little girl risked her life during the blackout to save her family and we want to talk to her," the reporter replied.

"It was no big deal," I say.

"Oh, yes, it was!" Sabin says loudly. "Sassy saved me big-time!"

Daddy grins and squeezes my hand. "Our Little Sister, our Sassy, is the woman of the hour!"

I've never heard anybody call me a woman before. I feel really tall.

"Sometimes the best things come in small packages," Grammy adds quietly. She gives me a big smile.

The photographer snaps pictures of all of us. *Click, click, click.*

Then the reporter asks me lots of questions.

"What's your name?"

"Sassy Simone Sanford."

"How old are you?"

"Nine and a half."

"How did you get out of the elevator?"

"I squeezed."

"Why were you chosen to be the rescuer of your family?"

"Because I'm the smallest. Everybody else was too big. I was the only one who could fit through the door."

"Were you afraid?"

I pause. "I was a little scared of the dark," I admit.

The photographer gets more pictures of our family.

I notice he takes lots of photos of Sadora and not very many of Sabin. When the news people finally realize our family is not very exciting, they pack up their gear and rush to the next emergency.

We walk slowly to the parking lot, pile back into our car, and drive home quietly. When we finally get home, I drop off to sleep right away. What a night!

CHAPTER THIRTEEN

Surprises

The next morning, I wake up early because I know Grammy will be heading for the airport in a few hours. I hurry down the stairs to grab some breakfast. Nobody else seems to be up.

But Grammy sits at the kitchen table, reading the morning newspaper and eating a bowl of granola cereal with blueberries and bananas on it. She makes even healthy stuff look yummy.

"Good morning. How's my little hero girl?" Grammy greets me with a smile. "Want some blueberries?"

"Hi, Grammy," I say. I give her a hug. "I'll have a banana, and I'm no hero. Actually, I think Sabin ought to get a prize for not wetting his pants!" We both laugh.

"Well, the paper says you're a superstar," Grammy tells me quietly. She continues to spoon her cereal into her mouth.

"What paper?"

"The morning newspaper right here." She nods toward the paper in front of her.

"I'm in the newspaper?"

"We all are."

"No way!"

"Way." Grammy grins at me.

I grab the paper. Page one is full of stories about wars and gas prices and the blackout. I don't see anything about our family.

"You're teasing me," I say to Grammy.

"Turn to page two," she says. She rinses out her cereal bowl.

I flip to the next page and almost drop the whole thing. In the middle of the page is a fuzzy black-and-white photo of me!

I'm grinning and looking a little goofy. My white dress looks really pretty, even though it looks a little dirty.

Under the picture the caption reads, LITTLE SISTER SAVES FAMILY.

"This is really funny," I tell Grammy. "Even the newspaper calls me Little Sister!"

The rest of the story is very short, but it's all about how I had crawled through the gap and gone for help. I can't believe it!

Sassy Sanford, the youngest child and smallest of three siblings, became a hero last night during our city's power emergency. When her family got trapped in an elevator, she was the only one who was small enough to climb through the partially opened door. She ran alone through the darkness to find help, and because of her efforts, her family was rescued quickly and safely. No one was injured.

The story doesn't mention anyone else's name, not even Mr. Williams. And of all the pictures of Sadora that had been taken the night before, the only photo to show up in the paper is the one of me in a dirty dress.

"Wow, Grammy," I say in amazement. "Wait till the kids at school see this!"

"I'm very proud of you, Sassy," she says as she hugs me again. "And the rest of your family are as well."

"I really didn't do very much," I tell her.

"You did what no one else could have done," Grammy reminds me. "That's all that counts."

I nibble on my banana and read the story once more. All the articles on that page are about the blackout.

BABY BORN IN TAXICAB DURING BLACKOUT! is at the top of the page.

HOSPITAL USES EMERGENCY GENERATORS is another story.

HIGH SCHOOL BASKETBALL GAME PLAYED BY CANDLE-LIGHT, another story reports. Cool stuff.

And one story about me and my family. Awesome.

The rest of the family finally trickles in for breakfast.

"This is so cool!" Daddy says as he reads the article. "I'm going to buy ten copies of today's paper!"

"Get twenty," Mom says as she fixes breakfast. "I'm sending this to everybody I know!"

"Hey, really cool, Sassy," Sadora tells me.

"You don't care they didn't use your picture?" I ask her, amazed she's not upset about that.

"You were the one who saved us, kid," she admits. Then she gobbles the rest of my banana.

"I'm just glad they forgot to mention me and my bathroom problems!" Sabin announces with relief after he reads the story.

I guess we can't delay it any longer, so we head out to take Grammy back to the airport.

At the security area she hugs us all, then she takes each grandchild aside for a private word or two. She always gives each of us a small package before she leaves.

I wonder what it will be this time.

I don't know what she says to Sabin and Sadora, or what she gives them, but when she gets to me, she kneels down and says, "Your name is your song, Sassy. Remember that."

I'm not exactly sure what she means, but then she reaches down into her Grammy Bag and pulls out a small package wrapped in gold foil paper.

"Open it when you get home. I love you, Sassy!"

"I love you, too, Grammy!" I'm trying not to get all sniffly.

She waves and disappears into the crowd.

The drive home seems slower and longer than usual. Sabin and Sadora finger their gold-wrapped packages like I do, but nobody peeks.

When we get out of the car, I race to the bathroom and lock the door. I want complete privacy as I open my surprise.

Even though I'm excited, I don't rip the gold foil. I take

my time and slowly unwrap the paper. I find not one, but two most wonderful things.

The first is a small, shiny plaque from The Name Store in the mall. Decorated with plastic diamonds and rubies around the edge, the letters in my name are written in gold sparkles. It's just perfect!

I hug it and grin. Grammy *always* knows what I need!

The second item is even smaller. It's a soft-pink key chain. On it is a tag made of shiny pink enamel. In bright gold letters, engraved on one side, is the word SASSY. On the other side, it says LITTLE SISTER.

A little note is attached. I take my time and read it slowly.

Dear Sassy,

The plaque is for your bedroom door and the key chain is for your Sassy Sack. The sparkly part of you can never hide under plain brown wrapping paper. Everyone knows it's there. To me you will always sparkle and shine like a jewel. I love you.

Grammy

I'm starting to get sniffly again. I blow my nose with toilet paper.

Sadora knocks on the bathroom door impatiently. "Hurry up, Sassy!" she cries. "I gotta go!"

I take my time, unlock the bathroom, and she rushes in. I think she wants privacy to open her gift as well.

I proudly hang my new sign on my bedroom door.

THIS ROOM BELONGS TO SASSY SIMONE

ALSO KNOWN AS

LITTLE SISTER

I carefully place the pink key chain in a zippered pocket of my Sassy Sack. I touch the sack gently. Every thread, every sparkle, every shiny button reminds me of Grammy. I miss her already. I can't wait until summer when I see her again.

Then I rush to the phone to call Jasmine. We have so much to talk about. Getting stuck in an elevator. My picture in the paper! I can't wait to see her at school tomorrow. I want to stand back-to-back and check our heights. I think I might be just a little taller.

About the Author

Sharon M. Draper is the acclaimed author of many books for young people, including *Copper Sun* and *Forged by Fire,* both winners of the Coretta Scott King Author Award. She has also written the popular Ziggy and the Black Dinosaurs series and *The Battle of Jericho,* a Coretta Scott King Honor Book. Ms. Draper was the 1997 National Teacher of the Year and has been honored at the White House six times. A highly respected educator and speaker, she has devoted her life to increasing literacy among young people. Ms. Draper lives in Cincinnati, Ohio, with her husband. She says, "When I was a little girl, I was a dreamer and a reader like Sassy. I wish I'd had a Sparkle Sack like Sassy's! It might have made my dreams come true."